Made in the USA
Monee, IL
19 March 2022

93130033R00073